Megan Louise Brierley loves escaping into the world of books through reading and writing. She is passionate about English Literature and History. In her spare time, Megan enjoys playing the flute and saxophone.

For the brightest star in the sky, I hope I've made you proud.

Megan Louise Brierley

LOVE AT SECOND SIGHT

Megan X

AUSTIN MACAULEY PUBLISHERS™

LONDON • CAMBRIDGE • NEW YORK • SHARJAH

A CIP catalogue record for this title is available from the British Library.

ISBN 9781035813674 (Paperback)
ISBN 9781035813681 (ePub e-book)

www.austinmacauley.com

First Published 2023
Austin Macauley Publishers Ltd®
1 Canada Square
Canary Wharf
London
E14 5AA

Firstly, thank you to everyone at Austin Macauley who was involved in publishing this book, it really wouldn't have happened without you!

Thank you to all of my amazing friends for your continuous support, you all know who you are. Emily, thank you for making me promise to never give up, I'm now on your bookshelf! Phoebe, I'd be so lost without you. Thank you for sticking by my side, love you, bestie.

Thanks also to all of my brilliant family for always believing in me. Mum, thanks for making me realise that my dream could come true, for encouraging me to persevere and for always putting up with my craziness, it can't be easy!

Dad, thank you for making good coffee, explaining what I don't understand and for knowing just what I need. I love you both. Toby, you're the best little brother, even if you're taller than me now! Thank you for making me laugh daily, please never stop.

Part One

Chapter One

I breathed out a sigh of relief as I exited the sparkling clean glass doors of the office I worked in. I was an administrative assistant of Ruddford & Co., although I wasn't entirely sure why the co was still in the title, as Max Ruddford (my snotty boss) had managed to drive away his 'co' due to his snotty ways.

He was a large, burly, spiteful man who never had a lack of saliva to spit in your direction when speaking to you and always seemed to have a cup of coffee (two sugars, drop of milk) sat on his desk going cold. You would have thought that with how stuck-up he was, his mouth would have been able to cope with scalding hot coffee, but no, he didn't even drink it when it was lukewarm. Disgusting! He was rather intimidating but, having worked in his business for the last five years, he didn't scare me.

I didn't do anything exciting there, but I took the job as a way of getting a life for myself. I finished my university degree (communications – completely and utterly boring) then left my hometown of Leeds and got myself a job and flat in Westminster, Central London.

It was nice getting away from the constant flapping of my mother, who always had something to say about planning a life for myself. The truth was, and always had been, that I didn't have a clue what to do with it. I had never been adventurous and had always been happy curled on the chair with my nose stuck in a book. It would be nice to earn a decent living from reading! All I knew I wanted from life was to leave home. I wanted to escape from the scrutiny from my family and leave behind the disappointment that they always struggled to hide. The only time they hadn't been disappointed was when I got straight As in my GCSEs, and that was only because my mum didn't let me do anything leisurely until I had revised for at least an hour a day. I wanted to be on my own, or at least with people of my choosing, who wouldn't judge me. I also wanted to be able to sit on the sofa with a packet of biscuits and eat each and every one of them without somebody reminding me of my waistline.

It was certainly nice living alone.

My job mostly consisted of answering the well-used phone that was on my pen-and-coffee-stained desk and put whoever was ringing through to the right person. I also got coffee on demand for Snotty-Boss as he seemed to forget that he had a PA (who just sat at her desk texting and probably looking at stuff that shouldn't be looked at in a workplace, due to the disgustingly smitten grin that sometimes spread over her face) whose job was literally to do what he asked her, including getting him coffee.

But I was free for a weekend. I didn't have to go back for a day's work until Monday, and it was only Thursday. I was going on a weekend away with my best friend, Jody, and I could not wait.

She had stayed in Leeds after university and was a primary school teacher, but, because I moved to London, we could no longer see each other as often, so we were going to Staithes – which was in North Yorkshire – for the weekend.

Me and Jody had grown up together, had been best friends since we were in playgroup. We did everything together as kids, always at each other's houses after school, and we even managed to bribe my mum to let us 'revise' together during high school so that we could see each other more.

I walked along the streets of Westminster back to my flat feeling excited and carefree. It was a poky little place on top of a small Italian restaurant on a narrow, cobbled street, which was owned by a lovely man who was just slightly crazy. The streets all merged into one as I took the well-known route back home, breathing in the familiar smells of Central London.

"Ciao, Miss Thorne," the Italian restaurant owner called to me as I came to a halt outside the door that led to my flat, the scent of citrus and limoncello filling my nose. He was busy watering the flowers in the planters outside the restaurant.

"Hi, Alessandro," I replied, unnecessarily and unusually cheerfully.

I think he was shocked by how happy I sounded as he almost dropped the watering can in the process of giving me a questionable one-eyebrow-up look, as if to say, 'what have you done with Sinead Thorne?'

I unlocked the downstairs door to my flat, after fumbling around in my bag for the key for what felt like decades, and ran up the stairs to the top door. This was the door that I liked to call my 'front door' because it was a nice, homely-feel door, unlike the depressing, chipped, ugly downstairs door. This door was mint green, a refreshing colour, and I had put a heart shaped driftwood wreath on it. I (as crazy and as stupid as it sounds) loved my 'front door' so much that I had found a matching mint ribbon that I had knotted around the keyring on my keys. Sad, I know!

It was nice going back home after a long day in the office. But, to some at least, my flat wasn't really a home by normal standards. It had three rooms: the kitchen and living room, which were combined into one room, my bedroom and the bathroom. It had been dull and all painted magnolia when I moved in (five years ago), so I had gone to the DIY shop and bought some tins of paint. I now had a kitchen wall painted bright yellow and a pastel blue bedroom. It made me happy even if it would cause others to question my sanity, of which there was the minimum amount someone needed to get by. My bathroom was the same grey tiles that were there when I moved in, but after a good few days of scrubbing on them they had become mostly limescale free.

After hanging my coat and bag on the hook on the wall, I freed my feet from the restraints of my black court heels and plodded over to the kitchen and made a cup of tea.

I took it with me into my bedroom and packed for the weekend. As much as I would love to say I was a messy, spontaneous packer, such as the likes of Bridget Jones, I had to do things in a certain order, so that I knew I had packed enough of everything and enough spares. I then had to neatly roll everything so that I knew they wouldn't get creased. As much as it used to annoy me that I couldn't be as spontaneous as book and film characters, now I like how insanely tidy and organised I am when it comes to packing, because at least then I have peace of mind that I have everything.

When I had finished, I laid on my bed, sipped on my tea and flicked through my phone. As I was doing so, my mum started WhatsApp video calling me. My older sister, Kate, had shown her how to do so which meant I had to put up with lectures on how I was choosing to live my life. Kate was Mum's idea of a 'perfect daughter'. She hadn't said so but it was obvious with the way she always praised her and told the neighbours about what was happening in Kate's life and not mine. Kate was married, had a two-year-old daughter called Bethany and was assistant manager of a firm. I lived in a poky flat on a cobbled street in London and was an administrative assistant.

Even though I just said that snarky stuff about her though, it doesn't mean we don't get along. After Jody, Kate is my closest friend. I tell her everything that happens in my life, and she never tells Mum. She also loads on me when she gets constant praise from Mum, but told what she needs to do now to make her life even better. She hates that whatever she does isn't good enough for her. Mum has said to her on multiple occasions that maybe she should try for another baby now that Bethany is two (she doesn't know the struggle that her and her husband, Cole, had to have Bethany, and didn't put up with hours of her crying when she had given up hope for a while) and that maybe now she has enough money saved up from her high-paying salary, she should quit work and become a stay-at-home mum for Bethany (yet she hasn't heard the weeping from the other end of the phone when the Mum guilt kicks in that she isn't doing everything right, which all grows from tiny seeds that Mum plants in her brain). It's safe to say that no matter how much someone is achieving in life, or how well they seem to be doing in her books, it's never good enough for her. But me and Kate are really close, and we always offload on one another when she has suggestions of better ways for us to live.

Whilst complaining about my mother, I think I should clear up that my dad is one of the best human beings I know. He is understanding, sweet and supportive and I couldn't ask for a better father. Sometimes, I genuinely wonder how he puts up with my mum, but I guess he must manage to calm her down somehow.

I accepted Mum's phone call, knowing full well I would be interrogated on my recent life choices, and lectured at my lack of desire to do anything about them.

"Hi, Sinead," called Mum.

"Hi, Mum."

"What have you being doing?"

"I've just packed for my weekend with Jody and now I'm drinking a cup of tea and talking to you."

"I hope it's not got any sugar in it, it would completely ruin your body you know. You still want to be able to fit into your clothes."

I inwardly rolled my eyes at her.

"Anyway," she continued, "how is Jody, is she still with Beck?"

"Yes, she is."

"Do you have any boyfriend yet?"

"No, Mum."

I inwardly eyerolled again as she went into another lecture about how I wasn't going to stay young forever.

The only long-term relationship I had was with my fridge and wine. I hadn't had a boyfriend worth mentioning since Aaron. We had been friends since primary school then grew closer in year ten. We stayed together until shortly after we finished university, when he got a job in America and long-distance didn't work for us. To be honest, we were stupid to not go somewhere together because he went to America and instead of going to London to look for jobs, I could have followed him to America. After all, we had been together for eight years. But I didn't and instead I was in London, lonely and still being lectured by my mum. I missed him though. I missed feeling protected as he held me in one of his tight hugs, which he only reserved for special people. It was stupid to miss him because we had split five years ago. We had agreed to stay friends, there wasn't an argument, it just seemed more sensible and mature to call it quits to prevent the sadness that came from being kept away from your love. We hadn't spoken in about three years though: eventually the messages of checking in on each other had stopped. He had got a new girlfriend; she was American and hadn't moved, so was in the same country as him. She didn't stupidly move a twelve-hour flight away from him. It may be safe to say, though, that I had never fully gotten over him.

Beck and Jody had been together for five years, since me and Jody left university, and they had moved in together the previous year. They were happy together and I was happy for them. They certainly were the most perfect couple, and they could most definitely post #couplegoals along with the cutesy images of them exploring beaches and drinking nightcaps on Instagram.

I got off WhatsApp as quick as possible, once Mum had finished her lectures on my life choices of course, and I threw together some tomato and pasta for my tea, mostly in spite of her, because it wasn't one of the lovingly homemade meals

17

she suggests for me. Who would cook something that can take up to three hours to make just for one person, when the hundred grams of spinach you're told to use wilts down to nothing in a matter of minutes? There is literally pasta that can be cooked in eight minutes, and voila, you have a perfectly nice meal! In order to spite her even more, I sat on the sofa and watched tv whilst eating – completely and utterly scandalous – and did my best to block out the world, specifically mothers and America.

Chapter Two

I was awoken the following morning by the familiar beeping of my alarm clock. It was six in the morning. At some point the evening before I had taken myself from my sofa to my bed, but I wasn't sure what time. Even though I was on holiday from work I still had to get up early. There's no rest for the wicked! Me and Jody had agreed to meet at the cottage we were renting for the weekend between 12 and 1 pm, which meant I had to be up at 6 and ready to set off at 7, because google maps had informed me that it would take 4 hours and 56 minutes for me to drive to Staithes.

I was sluggish and groggy and wanted to go back to sleep as I turned my alarm off, but then I remembered that it was the day I was going to see Jody, and I launched myself out of bed. It quickly changed me from being groggy to being bubbly and completely ecstatic.

I got ready with a new-found speed and excitement. I chose to wear a navy-blue floral dress and sandals. After all, it was mid-August.

I made toast and tea for breakfast, all the while the adrenaline and butterflies flowing through me, making me dance about like a completely insane woman. Well, I would usually do that anyway, but we'll ignore that.

I was so excited that I didn't care I'd burnt half of my mouth on my tea in my mad rush to get to Staithes. I washed and dried up, texted Jody I was about to set off, then hauled my suitcase and handbag out of the top door (checking three times that I had locked it), down the stairs, out of the bottom door, onto the cobbled street, then into the boot of my duck-egg blue Mini Cooper. Of course I frantically ran back up the stairs to check that I had locked the door again, then locked the bottom door, then set off on my way to Staithes.

*

Thankfully, there wasn't much traffic on the drive. Well, once I had gotten out of London of course! Staithes wasn't a difficult village to find so, approximately five hours later, at 12 pm, I parked on the street of the rented cottage and found Jody's red Hyundai parked up already.

I glimpsed up at the cottage and was instantly taken away by its beauty: there was a small, neat, cream-coloured picket fence, which was enclosing slightly overgrown green grass. The grass was beautifully dotted with lovely wildflower, all pink and blue and purple and yellow in colour. In the middle of the grass was a stone path, which led up to the navy-blue door. On either edge of the door was a hanging basket, with beautiful trailing flowers peeping over the edges. There was unruly, trailing, decorative ivy carelessly climbing up the walls of the house, reaching up to meet with the wooden cream panes of the windows and the dark grey slate tiles of the roof. It was very picturesque and beautiful, and out of nowhere my stomach did more gymnastics at the thought of spending a whole weekend there with my best friend – eek!

Jody must have been as excited as me because, as I was locking my car, she ran down the path with her arms outstretched.

I put my keys into my bag, which I had resting on my shoulder, and ran up to her.

We stood for a good few minutes in the middle of the pavement (yes, I know, an inconvenient spot but there wasn't anyone wanting to get past us) with our arms wrapped around each other, and each of us wondering how we managed to survive this long without the other.

It felt so good to be back with my best friend. She was the one person who I could always count on to be non-judgemental or give me great advice when my head turned into a foggy storm, whirling different bits of information around so that I couldn't think straight. I am so grateful that our paths crossed and we found each other: I would be completely lost without her.

"Oh my god, I've missed you!" Jody wailed as we slowly pulled away from our embrace.

"Not as much as I've missed you," I teased.

"Right, I'm starving, fancy a walk down into the main part of the village and grabbing a sandwich?"

"Yes!" I suddenly realised how hungry I was. All my attention had been on the excitement of seeing Jody that I hadn't noticed the growling of my stomach. It was like a tiger snarling at its prey.

We walked in the direction that the signs posted to the main village. To get to it, you had to walk down a humongous, steep, cobbled hill. It filled me with fear and dread on how we were going to make it down, but then how in hell were we to get back up after? Downhill is easier than uphill and if we could only just make it down the hill we didn't stand a chance getting back up. Still, if other people could do it, so could we.

A lesson to self to not wear sandals that rub on your feet!

But, eventually, I didn't care about the pain soaring through my feet and shins. I didn't care about the pain flying through my knees from the pressure of walking down the hill. I also didn't care about the burning in my lungs and throat at having to follow fitness fanatic Jody down. She was a remarkably fast walker. It was probably because of all the cardio she put herself through, not the lack of exercise or salad I had, I tried to convince myself. I didn't get the point of cardio, I wasn't unfit or unhealthy, so I wasn't going to put myself through unnecessary stuff if I didn't have to. The only thing it would cause in me was regret at doing it, as I would undoubtedly ache more after than I would before.

At last, we came to the bottom of the hill. We found a cafe and bought a sandwich wedge to take out each, then strolled along to the beach and sat on a bench eating them.

It was lovely to be sat under a blue sky with just a few clouds blanketing it. Gulls flew above us, or perched on the sand eating discarded fish and chips and dropped ice cream cones, all the while calling noisily to each other. There were families with young children who were screaming loudly in joy whilst building sandcastles; young couples strolling along, their hands entwined; older couples sat on foldable garden chairs eating ice creams, and teenagers trying to get a decent tan. It was lovely and peaceful and a very welcome break from London and work.

Once our sandwiches were finished, we sat for a bit longer, taking in the sunny weather and chatting.

"Okay," began Jody, "I have big news."

"Right, go on then," I said nervously, panic seeping through me. To me 'big news' didn't seem good, it sounded like something was going wrong. This was unhelpfully amplified by Jody being wary, as if worrying she could somehow upset me with what she had to tell me.

"Okay, I'm engaged!" she shrieked, so loudly that the other side of the world had the chance of hearing it.

She held up her left hand, which now adorned a thin, silver band with a small, dainty, sparkling diamond in the middle. It was utterly gorgeous and so completely Jody.

"Oh my goodness, congratulations Jody. Tell me everything!"

"Well, it was two weeks ago and Beck told me to put my nicest dress on, so I wore the red knee length one and he put on a proper suit with a cloth in the pocket and everything, so I suspected something was going to happen, but not a proposal! He ordered a taxi and we were driven to the Italian restaurant in the town centre. He had a reservation for a small two seated table by the window, which was slightly away from the other tables. I had spaghetti carbonara, as usual, and he had some pizza and we had expensive champagne, not the cheap stuff. Then, after we had finished our main course, a really beautiful instrumental song came on and that was when he got down on one knee with a ring box and asked me to marry him. I said yes straight away, well after I had practically burst, and then we danced for the rest of the song without caring about the rest of the people in the restaurant who may have been looking at us. They did all cheer when I said yes though! Oh, Sinead, it was so romantic and beautiful and just perfect! I couldn't sleep and kept checking my finger for my ring, just to remind myself of how wonderful it all was. I'm going to be Mrs Winter!"

She stopped to take a huge gulp of air: she had barely breathed throughout the whole story, except when she was forced to stop by my constant 'oohing' and 'aahing'.

It was beautiful and my insides melted as she told me. I was so happy for them both, they were wonderful together and he made her so cheery and pleased.

"That is just simply amazing, Jody! I am so happy for you. Oh my gosh, you have a wedding to plan!" I said.

"I'm glad you're happy for us. I wasn't sure how you would take it with you being single and me engaged, but I'm not going to mention that any further as it would remind you then. You have no idea how hard it has been to not tell you, but I wanted to keep it a secret to tell you now! Also, Sinead, please would you be my maid of honour?"

It seemed that all at once my jaw dropped to the floor and my mouth spread into a smile so wide that it went past my eyes – the worst Cheshire Cat impression ever. To be her maid of honour, what a privilege! I mean, when we were younger and had fantasised about our weddings, we had said we would be maid of honour for each other, but it was so real when it was actually happening. I absolutely wanted to do it!

"Yes, of course, thank you so much!"

"Oh, thank you for saying yes. It will be such a great day. We're planning for next August, so we have around a year."

"Ooh that sounds nice. It will be a great day just as long as I don't get hideously drunk and ruin all of the dancing with my embarrassing moves as I tended to have the habit of doing when we went on nights out!"

Then we both burst into fits of giggles at the fond memories of when we were younger and carefree.

*

For the rest of the afternoon, we went on a walk. It was a set route that we found maps for and it went over the top of the village. It was an exhilarating feeling, walking on the dried, powdery mud path in between long, overgrown grass that brushed on our hands and legs as the basking sun beamed down on our sun-kissed faces. Well, that's what we believed, but knowing our luck we would be more like sunburnt tomatoes than a lovely golden tan. And to be perfectly honest, whilst Jody didn't struggle with walking up the hills, I was more like a sweaty mess with hair stuck across my forehead and creaking knees. But I felt amazing. It was great to be able to swap the stale, polluted air for crisp, clean, fresh country air, which carried the aroma of flowers and nature.

We got to the end of a hill, which was evidently the highest we were going to get, and peered over the top. The view was breath-taking. Spectacular. Stunning. I wanted to stop the clocks and stay there forever. Being on the top of a magnificent village, overlooking it, and surrounded by the wonderful gift of nature with Jody. We paused and took it in, the only sounds being that of my heavy breathing and the faint chirping of the birds as they sang beautiful tunes.

The rows of colourful terraced houses in pastel colours that lined the cobbled hill was gorgeous enough, but the beach swarmed with people and the sea where it met the sky was a priceless view. Almost worth the patch of sweat on the back of my dress.

"Right, shall we go back? It's half four now and we need to get back and eat some dinner," Jody said after a while of taking the view in, and a few selfies of us, of course.

"Oh, gosh, yeah. I didn't realise how late it had gotten."

We made our way down at a leisurely pace, enjoying as much of it as we could before we reached the main village again. Our shoes caused the stones and gravel to make a crunching sound beneath us as our feet walked heavily downhill and, as we neared closer to the village, the smell of sea salt fused with the fresh smell of pollen.

For dinner, we got a table in what appeared to be the main pub. It was moderately sized and dimly lit, with a bar stretching its way along one wall and the murmuring of a group of men in one corner, and occasional bursts of laughter from them, filled the silence that would otherwise have been, except for the music that was faintly playing through the speakers. There was a fair few tables that were sticky from the anti-bacterial spray used to clean them. The scent of lager hung in the clammy air. But, it was a typical village pub, with welcoming workers and a decent selection of drinks as well as food.

Me and Jody both ordered a burger, fries and onion rings and we shared a bottle of wine.

Due to the mammoth walk we had completed, even the smell of food was making us salivate, so that when our food eventually came, it was barely ten minutes before our plates were completely cleared. With our stomachs full, we leaned back on the comfy, cushioned chairs with our wine and chatted about wedding plans.

They were just ideas that Jody had brainstormed and created a board for on Pinterest. We were going to arrange a day for me to join her and her sister-in-law-to-be in Leeds to go dress shopping, which was something to look forward to before the big day. It was during a tedious conversation that Jody seemed to be having with herself about whether she preferred sage green or deep purple for the dresses that I heard it. A harsh, rough, but oddly comforting voice. It couldn't be though, could it? It was probably a similar voice to most other men. But I heard it again, and it sent the butterflies that had stopped fluttering to suddenly flutter again. It caused a hot, burning sensation to flow through my whole body. It made me go slightly dizzy for a few seconds.

I looked over to where I heard it come from. He was over in the corner.

It was him.

He was there.

And I was here.

I could still hear Jody babbling on about something, but I wasn't listening. Instead I was listening to the sound of the man I once loved with all of my being and have never stopped loving. Jody seemed unaware of my distraction anyway.

I continued to stare at him. To listen to his voice, still familiar to me after all of the years that had passed.

Cautiously, as if he was scared of something, he glanced over his shoulder towards my direction, then back to his mates. Then, doing a double take, he turned his whole body to me. The hot rush happened all over again.

He started slowly walking towards me.

I anxiously stood up.

He walked to me faster now, appearing to be sure of himself.

I walked the few paces left to him.

27

"Sinead," he said.

"Aaron," I replied.

And then, as if by magic or some kind of fate, Whitney Houston's cover of *I Will Always Love You* started playing through the speakers. It is the song we danced to and shared our first kiss to. The song that held so many memories for our love that was broken.

Without giving it a second thought, he grabbed my waist and pulled me to him and we danced. His touch sent sparks through my body; it was like electricity. The feelings I had spent so long trying to bury, which I had eventually succeeded at doing, all came rushing back to me.

I looked up at him and his piercing green eyes which gently complimented his messy brown hair, and he gazed back into my eyes.

"I thought you had a new girlfriend," I whispered, as our hands were still around each other.

"I did, I broke up with her."

"You broke up with her? Why?"

"Because, Sinead, she wasn't you."

The electricity went wild, sending sparks all through me. Nothing else mattered except me, Aaron and the song.

"Sinead," he whispered, "I still love you."

"I still love you too," I whispered back.

I lay my head on his warm chest, let his hands rest on my hips, and felt safe and protected.

I had wished for so long that I had never let him go, but he was back and he had let someone go for me.

It was crazy how our paths had crossed again in the most unlikely of places, but it was perfect. Bizarre, yes, but oh so perfect.

Chapter Three

It was five in the morning; my phone told me. I hadn't slept though. I was completely and utterly bewildered as to what had happened. It was the morning after me and Aaron had danced to our song in the pub. His mates had headed back whilst we were dancing, Jody had stayed and watched us. Jody and Aaron were really close friends. He was welcomed into our little bubble when I became his girlfriend: he had never really had 'close friends' before that so was more than happy to hang out with us.

Once the song had finished, we had gone and sat back down at the table with Jody. We caught up on life. Aaron was living and working in London. As he had already informed me during the dance, he had broken up with his girlfriend and decided to move back. He said he didn't really enjoy the job there anyway, because even if you were out of the office you never really stopped working and he didn't want to live like that. So, he packed his bags and bought a flat in Holborn.

We had agreed for the three of us to meet in the same pub the next day for lunch to make up for lost time.

I originally felt guilty because it was a best friend getaway for me and Jody, but she seemed keen to see Aaron again, and of course she knew I still had feelings for him.

It sounds strange, but despite everything that had happened between us, nothing was awkward, it was as if nothing had changed. We were comfortable around each other and happy.

When we had finished chatting and drinking the second bottle of wine we had between us, we said our goodbyes to Aaron and walked back to the cottage. With the help of Jody, I got my suitcase from the boot of my Mini, up the narrow winding staircase of the cottage and into one of the small box rooms. Jody had gone straight to bed, appearing completely unfazed by what had happened. I, on the other hand, had been so wide awake from the events of the evening that I unpacked my clothes and hung them up on the tiny clothes rail on the wall, set out my makeup bag and hairbrushes on the little shelf which hung beneath it and made some coffee in the kitchen, which I took back up to my room so I could curl up under a blanket and read one of the books I had taken. I couldn't really concentrate on the book though, because I had so many questions flying through my head. If he had left another woman for me did that mean that we still stood a chance? If he was living in London then would a relationship now work? After all, we would no longer have the problem of distance. The thoughts were making me restless. Plus, I still had the sparks of electricity shooting through me.

Eventually, at about 2 am I must have dozed off, but I was awake again now, at 5 am, and still just as jubilant and enlivened as the night before. But, in the bright daylight that was streaming through the thin curtains, I could see the cottage properly. The room I was in had cream walls and the bed was made in a mustard yellow bedspread. The hallway was also cream and in a little corner was a wall shelf full to the brim with all genres of books and a mustard yellow armchair. A little book corner, something I had always wanted but had never had any room to have. I went into the marble tiled bathroom and got ready, then went back into my room and got dressed into my denim midi dress. I took extra care with my hair and makeup, after all I was seeing Aaron again, and the end result was a Sinead Thorne I barely recognised. I had never felt more jovial in my life.

Once ready, I walked down the pale grey carpeted, steep steps into the kitchen, where I found a hungover Jody sat at the table cradling a mug of strong coffee.

"Are you alright?" I asked her.

"Yes, just a bit too much wine," was her reply, in a remarkably rough voice.

We had drunk more or less the same amount, but I was way too elated to tell whether or not the lightheaded sensation going through me was an after-effect of the wine or seeing Aaron.

"Sinead, you're sure you still love him, aren't you?"

"Positive Jody, I never stopped loving him. Why?"

"Because this is the same guy who just buggered off to America without giving you or your relationship a second thought and then broke up with you and met another woman, only to dump her and come back to you."

"He dumped her because she wasn't me. And it wasn't like that. I told him to take the job because I didn't want to be a controlling girlfriend, and he didn't break up with me, we made the mature and sensible decision together to prevent more heartbreak in the future. Plus, this all happened in the space of, like, five years, so it's not as bad as you make it sound."

"Yes, but I remember when you first ended things with each other. You were heartbroken."

"But now he is back to mend my heart. You are close friends with him for God's sake, you know he would never mess me around. Not on purpose anyway."

"No, you're right. Sorry, I just don't want you getting hurt again. I actually don't remember the last time I saw you this happy."

"Yes, well you look a right state so you might want some painkillers and a shower."

"Oh, thank you. I try to give you a nice compliment."

And then we both burst into fits of giggles again and Jody went to get ready.

I put the kettle on to boil and looked around the place. It was a proper country cottage, beautifully decorated with a rustic feel.

The kitchen/dining room/living room were all in one open plan room. There was a rustic wooden television cabinet with a TV on top and DVDs in the glass-fronted cupboard below it. Next to it was a marble fireplace with a wooden framed mirror hanging above. Facing them both was a beige coloured sofa, which was filled with an assortment of cushions, from bright orange to muted grey.

Against the back wall was the kitchen cabinets, a stove and a fridge-freezer, and the wooden table and chairs were a couple of metres behind the sofa.

The floor was lightly stained wood and the walls were cream – decorated with paintings of farms and landscapes.

Whilst I was waiting for Jody to get ready, I ate some cereal that she had brought and drank a cup of tea, which I had made after the kettle had boiled.

Eventually, she emerged from upstairs with about half a bottle of foundation on and looking somewhat less hungover.

"Right, what are we going to do today?" she asked.

"I don't know. The sun is shining and we have a couple of hours to kill before we meet Aaron, so do you fancy just going on a stroll?"

"Yeah, sounds as good a plan as any."

So that is what we did. It was as peaceful and grounding as the day before, with the breeze gently wrapping around us and the sea air filling our lungs, ridding us of the clammy city air from Leeds and London. The view was just as nice too, absolutely breathtakingly beautiful.

We walked without an idea of where we were going, but sometimes those are the best walks. Just walking without thinking about the other a million and one things that come from being an adult, and just letting yourself feel young and like a teenager again.

That is what we were like, me and Jody: we were like teenagers again. That weekend had done the world of good for us. It was nice to just be carefree and how we used to be before we grew up.

I do believe, though, that you don't have to grow up. Not really. Yes, you do have to become 'an adult' and yes, you can never escape the wrinkles or cellulite or laughter lines. But that is what they are, marks on your body that are reminders of how much it has carried you through. Laughter lines that are reminders of the many days and nights spent laughing with friends and family, permanent reminders of happiness. Wrinkles and cellulite to prove how long you have survived, that even when you thought it was impossible you pulled through. All of these things are your body's way of saying "Look, you survived, and here is the proof."

I do believe that, although it may not always seem like it, you have a lot to thank your body for. Instead of cursing it and wishing yourself different, be grateful. Everyone is beautiful because everyone is different. Nobody can be compared against each other because they are not the same, there is nothing to compare.

I know I'm a fine one to talk about aging because I am still in my twenties, but age catches up with us all eventually and it is up to us whether we let it get to us, or whether we embrace it and tell it to go away, that its presence is unrequired. And to be honest, I prefer the latter.

*

We arrived at the pub later on to find Aaron sat at an outside table (which was facing the beach) and sipping a gin and tonic.

"Hey," he called to us when he had looked up and spotted us walking to him. "I didn't know how long you would be or what you wanted to drink so I didn't get you anything."

"Selfish," I joked with a playful smirk on my face.

"I'll go and get us two a G&T," Jody said to me.

Evidently, she hadn't learned her lesson from drinking alcohol after the state she was in that morning.

I began to sit down, rather gracefully at first, opposite Aaron, before managing, in true Sinead style, to bang my head on the parasol above us.

I sat down just as my face began to flush.

"Still the same clumsy Sinead then, I see," said Aaron, who seemed to find it exceedingly funny, at my expense.

His laugh, as infectious as ever, caused me to laugh as well, erasing the initial embarrassment.

I had originally been worried that there would be an elephant in the room, metaphorically of course, after the dance the evening before, but everything seemed fine. We were completely comfortable with each other and it was like we had never separated.

That dance had to mean something, didn't it? Also his words: no one makes a confession like that unless they truly mean it, do they? Was I stupid to look so deeply into it? He wasn't that drunk so they had to be heartfelt. But then what happened now? He made that confession and we danced, it had to lead to something, it just never stops there. It was like some kind of romance film; they break up and he comes running back. Except it wasn't a film or a book, and I had to think about what I would really want to come of it. That dance had made it all come back to me – cue *Celine Dion* singing – all of the feelings and thoughts and memories that we shared just reappeared after I had worked so hard to try and pick up the pieces when we split. He had to be feeling it too. But I wasn't making the first move. If he wanted me, and if he really did miss me, then he would. If he had left the other woman because she wasn't me then he would ask, just maybe when it was the two of us.

"Oi, what are you two laughing at without me?" Jody asked as she placed our drinks on the table.

"Oh, just Sinead being herself and banging her head on the parasol. We'd better check it for injuries actually, you could have hurt it, Sinead!"

"Oh, shut up you!" I exclaimed.

Yep, back to how it used to be, and with no awkwardness. Well, maybe a little on my part.

"Right, what are we getting for lunch?" asked Jody, always the one concerned about the lack of food in her stomach.

"Erm…" me and Aaron said in unison as we gazed at the menu.

We all got paninis in the end, after much contemplation, and they were very well received. We mostly talked about wedding plans (Jody was in a permanent state of wedding excitement) and the lack of excitement from her betrothed. Well, there wasn't lack of excitement, it's just that she was over the top.

Aaron did his best to appear interested but he wasn't overly bothered about deciding whether sage green or navy blue was a better feature colour, or whether lilies were better than roses for the bouquets.

But, it was a conversation at least, and it was better than silence.

After we had had lunch, me and Jody had strolled down to the beach, which was where we were now, soaking up the last few rays of sun and getting lost in the world of our books. She had always been a crime fiction fan, the bloodier and gorier it got the happier she was, but I was more of a lovey-dovey romance reader. At least reading about the romances made up for my lack of romance – in a way.

We had only a few hours left in Staithes, and it made me feel a bit depressed. I felt that I had truly taken a break from London life and I felt much happier and lighter after just a few days away. I think that is the effect good friends have on you though. Even after just a few hours with them, you feel like a different person.

Staithes was a truly wonderful place. All of the people were lovely, welcoming and genuine and the views were simply breathtaking. I loved everything about it. Except, of course, the hill that had to be walked up and down to get from the cottage to the main village. But everything else made up for that just about.

After we had been on the beach for a few hours and eaten fish and chips for our tea, me and Jody headed back up the hill (with much moaning from us both) and sat in front of the TV watching one of the DVDs that were in the cottage. As stupid as it sounds, we found *High School Musical* and decided to put it on for old times' sake. We used to watch it all the time when we were kids. God, we really had become our teenage selves again. Except we didn't have wine when we watched it as teenagers, no matter how many times we begged our parents.

Once it had finished, we went up to bed (letting our younger selves down slightly as they would have definitely stayed up longer) and that was it. It was mostly over. Back to Westminster the next day.

Chapter Four

I surprisingly slept well the last night in Staithes. Surprisingly because I had had so much excitement over the weekend, I had met my ex and it appeared that neither of us had truly gotten over each other, and stress about returning to work. I didn't want to see Snotty-Boss again, or become his PA even though he had one. I wanted a nice boss who understood my job title and what it actually included, instead of asking me to make them coffee when they feel like it.

Anyway, maybe it was the fact that the night before I hadn't really slept that well due to excitement about seeing and dancing with Aaron, and that I was lacking sleep so I slept well, despite not feeling that tired.

But, I woke feeling refreshed, probably good considering I had a five hour drive back to Westminster. I had already packed the night before, leaving just my hairbrush, makeup and toothbrush to put back in my case.

I got out of the cocoon of the pristine white bedsheets and plodded along to the bathroom to get ready. I opted for the last dress I had packed, a navy and white striped maxi dress, because I wasn't quite ready to go back to jeans and was trying to hold onto the heat in Staithes for a bit longer.

I made myself look less like a vampire and more alive by putting some make up on my face and running a brush through my hair, before putting the last bits in my suitcase and zipping it up.

I left my suitcase in the bedroom whilst I went downstairs for a cup of tea and some toast. I said a quick good morning to Jody, who then went upstairs to get ready whilst I ate breakfast. Once finished, I washed and dried up, made sure there was nothing of ours left, and hauled my suitcase downstairs and to my car.

I returned inside to find Jody wheeling her suitcase towards the door and trying to find her car keys to open her car.

Me – being the ever helpful and absolutely never sarcastic or irritating friend – found her car keys in the back pocket of her medium-blue jeans and opened her boot for her.

"Right, shall we just check the cottage and check we haven't left anything behind?" she asked.

"God, you sound like my mother, but yes. That's probably a good idea."

It turned out we hadn't left anything behind as Jody had feared.

As if time had just slipped away, it was time to say goodbye. It didn't feel fair that the two days had felt like two minutes, they had just flown by.

"Bye then, I guess," Jody whispered.

"Bye, Mrs Winter to be!"

"Ha! I'm going to miss you so much."

She leaped forward to give me a huge hug for a few minutes before we eventually pulled ourselves off each other, rather reluctantly.

The problem with growing up is that you can't just ring your best friend and see if they're free to meet you in 5 at your house. Instead, you end up living more or less five hours away from them and not able to drop everything to help them out if they have a problem. You end up relying on text messages and social media to stay in contact and only seeing each other once in a blue moon. Oh, the joys of growing up!

"I'll probably see you next for wedding dress shopping. I can't believe I'm getting married!" Jody exclaimed.

"Yes, text me the details so that we can try and find a date that I can do."

"Right, goodbye. Don't work too hard!" she said.

"Bye."

We embraced once more then both set off on our ways home.

*

The drive home was fairly peaceful again. I had my phone connected so all of my favourite songs had been blasting out and there wasn't much traffic. Well, maybe there was to some people, but obviously I was used to the hustle and bustle of London.

I got back to Westminster at 2, after stopping off at the service station for a sandwich for lunch.

I returned to my small, perfect flat and unpacked my suitcase. As I was putting on the washing machine, my phone pinged, alerting me to a text message that had come through.

I checked my phone.

It was Aaron.

Almost instantly, electric shocks ran through my body. My heart started going double time and I started shaking. It was a surprisingly enjoyable feeling. Was it normal to get so excited about a text message? Why was I having this reaction to him?

I checked the message. It read: *Hi Sinead, I'm back home in Holborn, I take it you might be back in Westminster as well. Fancy meeting up for a drink tonight? Aaron X*

Then my heart started doing triple time. I had to put my phone down on the worktop because my hands were shaking so much that I was at risk of dropping it. He put a kiss at the end of his message! That had to mean something, didn't it? Maybe, just maybe, my love life wasn't going to look so sad after all. Maybe, I had already found my happy ever after.

I was extra cautious about replying to his text, making sure that the damned autocorrect wasn't going to ruin any chances of me keeping my pride.

I typed back: *I would love to, where were you thinking and what time? Sinead X*

Then an exchange of messages unwound from there. It was agreed that he would pick me up from my place at seven, and we would go somewhere in Westminster.

I continued with the dreaded after-holiday-organisation with a new found spring in my step. I felt light and free, excited to see Aaron and only slightly nervous.

After I had unpacked and sorted everything out, I cleaned the whole of my flat, dusting, bleaching and hoovering everything until it was absolutely spotless and shining everywhere. If Aaron was picking me up, I wanted to make sure that it was clean and also I was too excited that I needed something to fill my time. It took me until half three. I still had three and a half hours until he was due to come.

I decided to spend that time trying to make myself look overly presentable, even though over the years we were together he had seen me at my best and my worst. I at least wanted to make sure that I looked like I had made an effort. I wanted him to feel like I cared.

I washed my hair, then wrapped it up in a hair towel whilst I put on makeup. I went for a neutral look that still made me look like I was wearing makeup and was quite pleased with the end result. Then, I dried my hair and curled it with my straighteners. It went really well and no hair was singed in the process. I was actually really happy with the way it turned out; I had soft curls framing my lightly blushed cheekbones and it made me feel pretty. Deciding what to wear was the hardest part.

After rifling through my wardrobe and pulling everything out, I looked just about presentable in a pale blue knee-length dress and tall navy heels (I was naturally quite short, so the whole boy-girl height difference wasn't an issue) but my floor was less so, with clothes thrown all over it. At least tidying gave me something to do.

I placed them all back onto hangers and put them back in my wardrobe and then hoovered my floor again.

It was 6. I still had an hour.

I ate a banana, thinking there could possibly be some food involved if we were going out so I didn't want to eat a meal before I went, but also not wanting my stomach to start growling out of hunger before we got a chance to.

When I had finished it, I brushed my teeth, being careful to not wipe my makeup, and reapplied my pale pink lip gloss.

It was half past six.

My phone pinged again. Instantly, my heart leaped back into double time, just when I thought that I had gotten it under control. It was Aaron.

Hey, do you fancy going a bit earlier, I'm ready to come for you now x

Absolutely x

I had replied.

So, I didn't have half an hour to wait. It was 15 minutes from Holborn to Westminster. I got my small black shoulder bag ready and put my heels on, then sat waiting.

*

At around 6:45, Aaron knocked on the door. We set off straight away, getting a taxi to where the bars were, and going into the first good one we saw.

I know it sounds reckless of me to have drinks the night before working again, but I had good self-control when it came to alcohol and I didn't have to worry about getting drunk. To my great surprise, Aaron had remembered I had work and ordered me mocktails as well. It was a bit awkward when people assumed that we were a couple and were pregnant and I just wasn't showing yet, but it didn't matter too much what people thought.

Eventually, we had got up to dance. We had spent a lot of time just sitting and chatting about nothing in particular and just life in general, but we had both – perhaps stupidly –

avoided the elephant in the room: our clear chemistry and attraction to each other. It wasn't awkward or anything, it just felt like there was something unsaid between us – just something we knew we needed to sort out, like paying the bills.

It wasn't until we had started dancing that we spoke about it.

We had moved to a different bar – a less rowdy one that had music that couples could slow dance to, and that is what most couples were doing, so we had decided to as well.

That didn't feel strange, it felt natural, perhaps because we had danced already since we met again.

So, we were slow dancing to a song that didn't sound familiar to me and Aaron was the one to break the ice.

"Sinead," he had begun, "I know that we have only just found each other again, but I think I speak for us both when I say there is still attraction. I hate myself for leaving you all those years ago, and I was a complete fool for thinking I could ever love anyone as much as I love you. So, Sinead, tell me to go away if you want, but do you think we could ever have something again?"

I felt like the world was spinning around me. Just his words and his voice could sent a warm, electric, heated sensation through me.

"Yes."

Knee-jerk reaction. The easiest yes I had ever said. It was as easy as dropping a hot object, or less drastic, breathing.

It was sorted. The metaphorical elephant in the room had disappeared.

Some people may judge and say that it was very soon after we had met again that this happened, but when you have been through what we had, and then had found each other again, it was as if the time in between didn't count. We didn't have to get to know each other, and we knew what we wanted.

As the song drew out its last bars, Aaron pulled me tighter into him and rested his head on mine. I rested my head on his familiar chest, breathed in the scent of his musky, astringent cologne.

And that is when my phone rang. It was my mum. I had originally rolled my eyes and replaced my phone into my bag. But then it started ringing again. This time it was Kate. Worry started to sink through me; something must have happened for them both to be ringing me.

Aaron must have sensed the worry.

"Sinead, are you ok?"

"I don't know, somethings not right. I'm just going outside to answer it."

"Ok, I'm here if you need me."

The walk from the bar to outside seemed to take an eternity, my legs threatening to give way beneath me the whole way. I left the bar and leaned against the brick exterior wall for support, the coldness of it was a refreshing sensation.

"Hi, Kate," I said as I answered the phone and brought it up to my ear.

"Sinead, where are you? You need to get to the hospital quick, it's Dad."

Worry struck though me like a knife. What had happened? Why was Dad in hospital? Was he going to be ok? My brain was working overtime whilst I tried to calm myself and coordinate what I had to do.

"I'm at a bar, I'm on my way," I said into the phone and then hung up.

I had gotten into such a state of shock that I didn't realise Aaron stood beside me.

"What is it, Sinead?"

"It's Dad. He's in hospital, I don't know why, I just have to get there."

My voice cracked as I said it whilst I tried to fight back tears.

"Do you need me?"

I couldn't even speak whilst I nodded with tears streaming down my face.

Aaron hailed a taxi and led me to it, holding my hand and pulling me against him to help me.

My whole body was shaking, I had never been so full of fear.

The whole ride there, I was imagining worst case scenarios in my head. It made me feel grateful that Aaron was next to me, protecting me.

"It will be ok," he whispered into my hair as he pulled my face against his chest.

He used his index finger to wipe under my eyes, getting rid of the tears but probably smudging my mascara. It was probably too late to dwell on smudged mascara anyway; I didn't care about how I looked, I just wanted to see my dad and make sure he was ok.

Aaron held me close the whole taxi ride. I spent most of it sobbing into his chest and trying to slow down my breathing. I felt as if I was hyperventilating. It was by far the scariest moment of my life.

After what felt like an eternity, the taxi pulled into the hospital drop-off section and, as I scrambled out, Aaron paid the driver.

We went to the main desk and asked where my dad was, then ran to find him.

Outside of the room where he was, Kate was stood pacing. So was Cole.

Bethany was presumably with Cole's parents.

Cole was there.

That was not a good sign. Something had to be seriously wrong if Cole couldn't stay at home to look after Bethany.

"Oh, I'm so glad you're here," Kate said, the relief showing in her tensed up body and puffy, red, tear-stained face.

She pulled me in for a hug, her body relaxing into mine.

She looked up and saw Aaron. Confusion initially flicked across her face, then something clicked in it and she must have realised we were giving things another go.

"I'm so glad you're here to support her," she said to him.

"Please tell me what the hell is going on Kate," I said.

She broke down in tears all over again.

"I can't be the one to tell you Sinead, I just can't."

She looked so fragile, as if just one accidental bump could shatter her petite body into pieces.

"I think it would be a good idea to go in, Mum is in there. The nurse will explain to you, I'll go get her," she said in between her blubs.

I hesitantly but meaningfully started to walk into the room.

My breath caught in my throat. I couldn't stand. I couldn't support my body weight. Aaron supportively put his hand on my shoulder.

"You can do this Sinead, you're one of the strongest people I know," he said, "if you need me, I'm right out here. Go on, go see your dad."

That was the boost I needed to get me through the door.

What met me on the other side was a sight I did not want to see.

My dad, ever so full of life and joy, was laid, pale and seemingly lifeless, on a hospital bed, hooked up with dozens of wires to various machines.

It was utterly heart-breaking.

Chapter Five

The nurse had told me what was happening.

Now I was sat with Aaron, Kate, Cole and Mum in Dad's room, all of us sat in chairs surrounding the bed.

I felt empty, like I had nothing in the world to be living for – completely numbed of all feeling and drained of any energy.

Aaron had kept checking everybody was happy for him to be there (I think he was conscious it was for family to be there) but I kept reminding him that we all already knew him so well from all the years before that it would be better if he was there for us all. Selfishly, I felt like I needed him to get me through this. It was like I had wiped the five years without him from my life and he would have been here to support me through this regardless.

Dad was dying.

We were told he probably wouldn't make it through the night.

And now it felt as if we were all here just waiting for it to happen. Or we were hanging onto the last ounce of life he had left.

He had been selfless up to his last hours.

Up until Mum had been forced to call the hospital, saying he really wasn't well.

At least she knew.

He had kept it from everyone else. Like I said, selfless.

Well in a way, at least.

He hadn't told us so that we wouldn't remember him fighting it.

There had been hope for a while, apparently.

He had thought he'd have longer: he was planning to tell us closer to the end, when we could still remember him being happy but only know how things would turn out to be at the last possible minute.

Instead, a nurse had told us whilst he was on his deathbed.

And here we were, all of us sobbing, my mother hunched over him, holding his hand and repeatedly whispering his name.

Cancer.

That's what it was.

They'd known a few months, had caught it late and knew there was no getting rid of it, but he thought he'd have a bit longer before he had to tell us.

But no.

Now I was sat, sobbing, trying to remember if I'd told him I love him the last time I saw him.

Cancer.

It's absolutely abhorrent.

Robbing people of their lives.

Tearing the people who love them apart.

Pancreatic cancer.

So difficult to detect, yet so aggressive and cruel.

Completely malevolent.

I have no words to describe how angry I was at it.

For robbing me and Kate of a dad; for robbing Cole and potentially Aaron of a father-in-law – for robbing Mum of a husband, and God forbid for robbing Bethany of a grandad.

Oh, poor little Bethany.

She had no clue what was going on. She had no clue how cruel the world could be. She had no clue that completely innocent people could just be ripped out of life as easily as pages from a book.

Why did it have to happen to him?

He was one of the kindest men on the planet, yet it happened to him. Why?

I was angry at everything I could be. Why did it have to be so clean? Everything was so sterile, the bed sheets crisp and white, the surfaces sprayed clean, the boring, plain floors and walls. It was like the universe was saying 'oh, we know this is the hardest time of your life and your dad is dying, but here is a clean hospital room for you to stay whilst it happens, we hope it makes up for your loss.' Why?

Sometimes, the world is just so fricking unfair.

The nurse came in to check some machines. She adjusted some things, wrote some things down, and then gave us all a pity smile. Yeah lady, like that was going to change anything.

"We've made sure he's comfortable so that he passes peacefully," she said calmly and sympathetically, "if we can get you anything do let us know, we're here to help you as well."

Oh, like some overpriced, rank hospital coffee would fix the situation.

I know they were only trying to be nice and they would have done a fantastic job of looking after Dad to make sure he had the best end to life, but when it feels the world is against you, you go targeting anything that you can.

*

It was 01.30 am when he passed.

It was peaceful, yet difficult.

I'll never forget the moment the beeping of the pulse detecting machine became one long, drawn out beep. Then it stopped. And there was silence. And there was the ear-piercing, heart-wrenching, love-sick wail of my mum as she positioned herself on the bed next to him, wrapping her arms around him and refusing to let him go.

I don't remember much else.

All I remember is kissing him goodbye on the forehead, squeezing his hand and telling him I love him.

I also remember Aaron pulling me close, not saying anything because he knew that nothing needed to be said, but holding me close and just letting me weep and wail.

And then I was laid in the bed in my parents' spare room. I don't remember how I got there. I knew that Aaron was laid next to me, holding me close around my waist and gently stroking my hair back off my forehead.

I rolled over and buried my face in his chest again.

"How did we get here?" I asked him.

"I got us all a taxi back. I'd had too much to drink to drive but I'll go back and get Kate's car today. You were out of it, couldn't even stand up, so I carried you up here. Kate sorted your mum out and Cole sorted Kate out."

"Thank you," I managed to whisper.

"No problem, I'm here for anything."

I didn't feel like doing anything. My face ached from crying and it felt puffy and swollen. I knew that I should help Kate with funeral arrangements, but I didn't have the energy for anything. I didn't even want to sleep. I just laid, not doing anything, thinking about how empty I felt without my dad.

*

I spent days like that not doing anything. I didn't even brush my teeth the day after, didn't shower until the third day, and even then Aaron had to help me by holding me up. I didn't even have the energy to contemplate how strange that seemed, but like I said, it was like there had never been the five year gap in our relationship.

Sometimes, people come into our lives for a reason. Maybe the universe knew he was the only one for me and I was the only one for him and that I would need him, so it made us cross paths.

I still don't know how I would have survived it without him.

It is because of him that I managed to eat something, drink something, shower and brush my teeth. He even brushed my hair for me.

After a few days, he made me get out of the spare room and downstairs. He told me I couldn't spend the rest of my life locked up there. He pulled me by the arm into the kitchen, where I found the breakfast bar swarmed with baking dishes of lasagne and casseroles. News travelled fast, and it seemed that everybody's first instinct was to make food. At least we didn't have to think about cooking.

I spent that day going through funeral arrangements with Kate. It was difficult, but I managed to get through it. And it was after that that I started to tell myself that I could do it, I could pull through the grief. I couldn't imagine it fully going away, but I could continue treading water until I was closer to the shore. Then I would no longer be drowning in it.

*

I did it.

I got back to the shore.

I helped Kate plan the funeral. I supported Mum. I washed my hair. I got dressed into clothes other than pyjamas. I even rang Jody. I went back to my flat. I survived. I ate more. I gave myself more kindness, more praise for getting through.

I got through the funeral. The second hardest day of my life. I smiled at people, spoke to people, listened to their memories and stories of my father, even the people I didn't know. I gave them no reason to give the bereaved daughter sympathy. I cried on Aaron's shoulder, but I raised my chin up again and continued.

I wrote a thank you letter to the nurses who looked after my dad. I spoke to my mum, actually spoke to her. I had meaningful, deep conversations with her. I came to realise that although I never really saw it, she did only want the best for me. I told her about my life and explained to her how much I loved it, and she told me she was proud of me. She told me she was proud of me! She saw my way of living and how I enjoyed it. She realised that I didn't need the things in life that she did to feel happy.

I spent more time with Aaron. I spent a lot of time with him. In fact, I spent most of my time with Aaron. We spent most nights at each other's flats, acting like we were the couple from five years before who had lived together for a bit. We were hardly ever apart. We made our relationship official. We proudly told people about each other.

I felt like I was drowning less and less.

It will never hurt any less though.

No matter what people tell you, the pain doesn't ever go away, that I can tell you upfront. But, little by little, day by day, you will find ways to heal the pain, you will find ways to cope when you feel like you are drowning. And eventually, you will find enjoyment in things you used to. You will see a photo of your loved one and cry happy tears for the memories you have with them – instead of sad tears for the loss of them. You find yourself telling stories of them when something reminds you of them. You will find relief from the pain. I promise you, no matter how hard it becomes, do not give up. Your pain will never go away, but you will become strong enough to fight it. You will get through it.

Part Two
Four Months Later – December

Chapter Six

I had thought I was past getting excited, that maybe as you grew older you didn't get excited. But Aaron somehow made me feel like I was seventeen all over again and experiencing love for the first time. Although, Aaron was my first love and we were just doing it again. Maybe it is love at first sight. Or maybe, as it seemed to be in our case, it is love at second sight, or perhaps love at first sight repeated.

Aaron most certainly made me feel giddy about love – giddy about him. I still felt a spark shoot through me when he touched or kissed me, like a firework exploding in the sky. It was a feeling I had never experienced with anyone else but him. We were hardly ever apart. We were always stopping over at each other's flats, cooking together, walking together and finding fun things to do together at the weekend when we were both off work. It was like we were magnets, no matter how far apart we were, we couldn't repel, we just attracted and ended up running back to each other.

He gave me a new outlook on life. I was bouncier, happier, and I could even tolerate Snotty-Boss when I went back to work after having some time off when my dad died.

I also thought that as you got older your excitement about weddings went away. Yet, it was the day we were going to

Leeds so that I could meet Jody and do the dress fittings. Somehow, I was more excited than we had gotten at sleepovers as kids when we would stop up late and imagine how our weddings would be.

Me and Aaron were driving down together as he and Beck were doing something sporty. I didn't remember what, because, if I'm totally honest, the word *football* was said and my brain switched off. But, there you go, at least I knew it was football! We had also planned that at the end of the day we would all meet back up and got out for a meal, basically a double date. Me and Aaron were staying in their spare bedroom and then driving back to London the following day.

*

I was sat next to Jody's mum and soon to be sister-in-law in the wedding dress shop feeling tired, sticky from sweat and bored. But that just made me feel guilty for feeling that at my best friend's wedding dress shopping. The truth was that no one ever spoke about how frustrating it could be. The air-conditioner was terrible, which left us feeling stuffy from the heat in the shop, even though it was mid-December. The prosecco tasted cheap and Jody was getting frustrated about not being able to find a dress she loved.

The day had initially started off great though. As soon as we had pulled onto Jody and Beck's street, they had opened the front door and walked to join us as we were stepping out of the car. We all hugged and greeted, then walked inside where there were steaming mugs of tea waiting for us.

I had always been envious of Jody's mugs, it seems silly to say, but as put together and organised as that woman was, she did not have a matching mug collection, which was the usual expectation. Instead, she had a cupboard full of mugs that she had collected over the years. So, my tea was in a Cheshire Cat mug and Aaron's was in a Cat in the Hat mug. Yes, her mug collection was truly insane.

Whilst we were drinking the tea, Jody's mum, Kathleen, and sister-in-law, Georgie, arrived, so once we had drunk it we set off on our way. Kathleen drove us to the shop after we had said goodbye to Beck and Aaron and left them to do whatever it was they were doing.

The car journey, which was all of ten minutes, had been filled with singing old classic songs from our childhood.

And then we had arrived at the shop. We were greeted by a most sweet lady who had prosecco poured already for us. She sat me, Kathleen and Georgie on a sofa and then took Jody, presumably to take her measurements for the dress and ask what sort of dress she wanted.

The shop was actually really pretty. The walls were painted white and the floor was a pale, grey, wooden herringbone pattern. There were shelves with vases of flowers, real and artificial, and the sides of the room were lined with rails of dresses from traditional white to pale pink. There were also some bridesmaids' dresses, which we may have been trying on later if Jody managed to find her dress.

It was a tedious process. It was just about lunchtime and she had so far tried on twelve dresses, aways finding something to criticise about it. I was starting to wonder whether people really did get the feeling that a dress was 'the one' or whether they just said it to make them feel like they had made the right choice of dress.

As we were starting to get hungry, we heard the familiar sound of the door at the back opening and Jody walking out. The dress was beautiful. We all drew in a sharp breath as she just about floated towards us and the mirror. We got the feeling that it was the one, we just hoped to goodness that she did as well.

It was an A-line dress with a lace skirt and a tight-fitting bodice that had thin straps.

Jody carried on heading towards the mirror and, after seeing our reaction to the dress, had a new found enthusiasm. As soon as she caught a sight of it she also had a sharp intake of breath. She had tears in her eyes as she turned around to face us.

"I think this is the one!" she exclaimed with a weak, emotional voice.

"So do we!" we all exclaimed in reply to her.

The shop assistant took her back through to the back room to check where alterations were needed.

Ok, you definitely knew when a dress was 'The One'. Whilst Jody had been trying to stay optimistic and find a good comment to say about each dress, there was just a look about her when she was wearing her chosen wedding dress. She was glowing and looked like she was floating towards us rather than walking. All of her best features were highlighted, and most importantly, we could see her wearing it on the big day.

Once she came back to join us, we went out for lunch – the smile she wore never once slipping from her mouth.

We sat in a small café on the end of the street that the dress shop was on and we all ordered toasted currant teacakes and tea.

Through the duration of lunch, Jody babbled on like a toddler about her various wedding plans, so there really was going to be no surprise for us on the wedding day. But I didn't mind; it was nice seeing her so happy and ecstatic about life.

Once we'd finished lunch, we went to look for bridesmaids' dresses. Surprisingly, this didn't take as long because she already had a big idea of what she wanted. The colour theme for the wedding was sage green, so we tried on the dresses of the shop had in that colour. We only had to try two dresses on, the first was deemed very old-fashioned, which I had to agree with, but the second was absolutely perfect. It was made of layers of tulle-like fabric wrapped around the bodice, and then subtly spreading out into a skirt. Although it wasn't my wedding, I did feel like a princess in the dress. It was definitely something I could attend my best friend's wedding in.

*

Jody, now satisfied with her dress choices, was gushing over how perfect the wedding would be (without trying to let slip what her dress was like) as me, Jody, Beck and Aaron were sat around the table in the restaurant. Beck and Aaron had had fun doing whatever it was they had done and had attempted to tell us about it but, as much as I loved the sound of his voice, I just couldn't find the concentration or patience to listen to what they had done. I'd just better keep everything crossed that he didn't ask me about it later!

I had the carefree, excitable, ready-to-conquer-the-world feeling that came from just taking a day off and spending it surrounded by people you love. I felt like the world had finally turned on its axis, that it had gone from hating me and being against me to being on my side and wanting things to work out for me.

Well, work out for me they had and I spent the rest of the evening and night with my friends smiling and laughing with delight, feeling forever grateful and thanking my lucky stars that things had turned out how they had done.

Chapter Seven

Christmas Day.

"One more, one more!" Aaron exclaimed to me as we sat in my poky flat in our cringy matching couple pyjamas.

"Alright," I moaned, hating how much he was spoiling me when I had had no clue what to get him. From me he had received ties and socks – the standard present.

So far he had got me wine, notebooks and pens, earrings, and a selection of random DVDs. I didn't know what else he could get me that I would love, but it seemed like I was about to find out.

He handed me the gift, which was a small box wrapped in shimmering pink wrapping paper. I was carefully peeling back the Sellotape holding it in place and gently sliding it off the box when Aaron's masculine hand snatched it away again.

It took me the whole half a second of lifting my head up to see him only to realise he was kneeled on the floor in front of me.

I bet you can guess what happened next, can't you? But, surprise, I'm going to tell you anyway!

The Christmas tree, decorated with shining silver baubles, tinsel, twinkling fairy lights, and pictures of me and Aaron looked beautiful directly behind where Aaron was kneeled.

The box that rested gently in his no doubt sweaty hand was blue and velvet, protecting the gorgeous ring sitting inside it.

"Sinead, I know that this would probably be a rush for a lot of other couples, but we both know that we seemingly get drawn back to each other, which my head can only think of one explanation for: we're meant to be together."

He paused to take a breath and swallow. All of my senses had heightened.

"I love you so much Sinead, and I would be stupid not to spend the rest of my life with you. Without you… my life is meaningless. Please, please, will you marry me?"

I couldn't answer at first; I had tears streaming down my face and my throat had closed up with emotion. But when I could speak, the answer came to me as naturally as breathing.

"Yes, yes, yes I will!" I replied, as he picked me up and spun me around.

Once he had put me back on the floor, he slid the ring onto my finger.

It took my breath away almost as much as he did. It was simply stunning. In the centre of the silver band, which was twisted to make it look like vines, was a silver rose with a small pink stone in the middle. It was meant to be a rose, the flower of romance, beauty, love and courage. I could not think of a nicer ring.

I would no longer be Miss Sinead Thorne, I would be Mrs Sinead Woodbury! Eek! The thought filled me with so much happiness and adrenaline. I got to spend a whole lifetime with the man I loved. I got to make all of the big life decisions with him, raise a family with him, get old with him. I was a bit biased, but I thought I was a fairly good competitor for the luckiest woman alive.

It truly was the best Christmas ever, and every Christmas after that one would be too, because it would be spent with Aaron.

Epilogue

That will be us soon, I thought, as I watched Jody and Beck exchange their vows. They'd picked a good day for a wedding, as the scorching August sun beat down on us through the church windows.

So, life had worked out well for me. Not only had I gotten engaged to the love of my life, but I had also got a new job! Crazy! A few weeks after Christmas, I saw a role advertised for a senior position in a publishing company, something I never really knew I was into, and Aaron gave me the confidence to do it. A couple of weeks after applying for it, I had an interview and then found out I had the job! I worked my notice period for Snotty-Boss, who subsequently wasn't happy that he had to find a new coffee bearer, but he would live or just learn how to make his own coffee. I didn't feel guilty somebody else would have to put up with him. I much preferred my new job, I got excited to go every day. It was no longer a burden and I had made some good friends out of my colleagues.

We had also found a house we were looking at putting an offer in for, as once we were married we wanted to move into a proper home, rather than just my flat, which Aaron had officially moved into after we'd got engaged. But there was no rush, it would all work itself out. As long as I had him, I was happy.

Sometimes, love at second sight really does work.

THE END